Anything but a Shot

For Kathie,
Who is and always will
be the love of my life.

My mom bought me an ice cream cone and then told me that I had to go to the doctor to get a shot. I thought it was going to be a pretty nice day...

until she told me what a shot was.

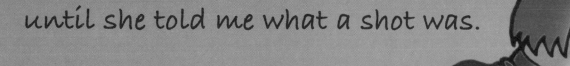

If I could, I would rather give an elephant a bath than get a shot.

I would rather talk to a llama than get a shot.

It would be better to arm-wrestle an octopus than to get a shot.

I would be happier
cleaning a giraffe's ears
than getting a shot.

If dinosaurs weren't extinct, I would rather put a tutu on a Tyrannosaurus Rex than get a shot.

It would probably be less painful to give a porcupine a backrub than to get a shot.

I would rather try to feed a snake than get a shot.

I would rather climb
a tree with a beaver
than get a shot.

I would rather pet an electric eel than get a shot.

If I had the choice, I would rather eat ticks off of a monkeys back than get a shot.

When I had finished telling the doctor why I was not going to get a shot, he just smiled and told me that while I was talking he had given me the shot. I didn't even notice!

Then the doctor gave me a lollipop for being so brave.

I guess that shots aren't too bad after all.

_____ would rather

Child's name

1. _____

2. _____

3. _____

than get a shot.